MW00953267

If you do what you love, life will make sense, despite any suffering you might face.

www.mascotbooks.com

Scromlette the Omelet Chef

For more information, please contact:
Mascot Books
620 Herndon Parkway #320
Herndon, VA 20170
info@mascotbooks.com

Library of Congress Control Number: 2020905061

CPSIA Code: PRTWP0720A
ISBN-13: 978-1-64543-413-9

Printed in South Korea

Scromlette the OMELET CHEF

Zach Christensen

illustrated by Chiara Civati

FLOUR

There once was a kid whose
Name was Scromlette.
And he could make a
Super mean omelet.

Scromlette was skinny
He was not buff
But when he cooked eggs
He took no guff

Scrom would use mushrooms,
peppers, avocados and lime
This kid cranked out breakfast
Any day, any time

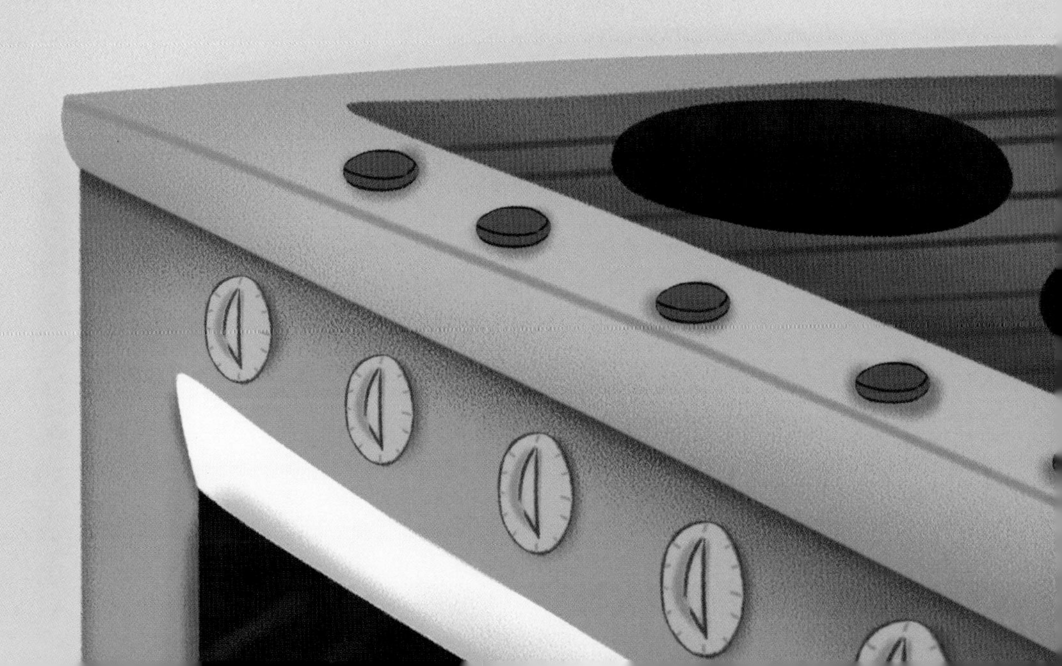

Scromlette went to school
And he worked hard
He had good grades
On each report card

But some kids were mean
They were not kind
They bullied people
Without a care
In their mind

Scromlette was picked on
Because he was small
He would get tripped
As he walked
Down the hall

He was called names
His feelings were hurt
He couldn't fight back
And he felt like dirt

But Scromlette kept cooking

Because that was his thing
Even though his heart hurt
Omelets made his heart sing

Scromlette grew up
He graduated from school
He pursued his dreams
Because he wasn't a fool

He studied to be a chef
Scrom wanted to be better
His omelets improved
Because he was a go-getter

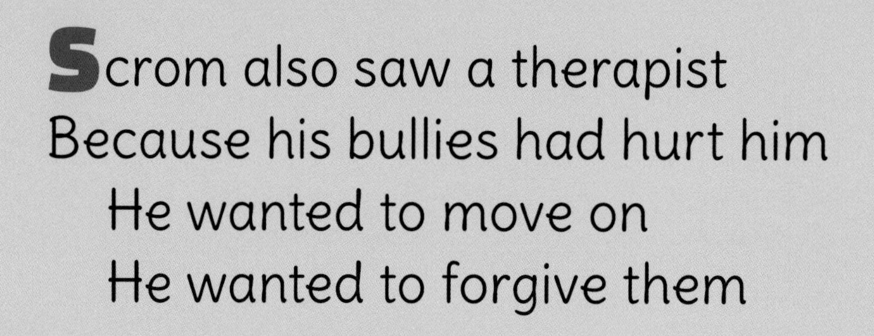

Scrom also saw a therapist
Because his bullies had hurt him
He wanted to move on
He wanted to forgive them

After time had passed
He stopped being bitter
He forgave them at last
Because he was no quitter

Scrom wanted to help people
In a world all helter skelter
He wanted to feed people
So he started his own homeless shelter

Scromlette was the head chef
And he led all the cooking
No one ever left hungry
Nor had they ever seen breakfast so good-looking

He made the best omelets ever
For those of humble estates
If people had empty pockets
He could serve them full plates

Scrom loved his life

He wouldn't change a thing
The stove was his kingdom
And he was the king

But the kids who bullied him
Were not doing so good
They dropped out of school
And never achieved what they could

They lived on the streets
Without a roof over their heads
They never had hot food
Or any warm, comfy beds

The bullies came to the shelter
On a cold winter night
They were too tired to work
And too hungry to fight

When the bullies saw Scromlette
They were totally shocked
They couldn't believe
Their eyes as they gawked

They were filled with fear
And they were full of dread
This kid they had picked on
Would decide if they got fed

"We are sorry for hurting you"

One bully said with tears
"It was wrong what we did
In school all those years"

The other bullies spoke up
With their voices hoarse
And each of them showed
A clear sense of remorse

"We were never cared for
By fathers and mothers
We only felt safe
When we could hurt others"

The bullies felt bad
For what they had done
    They were out on their own
    With nowhere to run

The bullies knew
What they had done was wrong
    And they finally saw
    That Scromlette was strong

Then Scromlette said

“Your apology means a lot

Now that you’re here
I can share a thought”

“As I hear your words
And understand what you say
Now I can see
Why you acted that way”

"I have already forgiven you
I already let it go
Because if I stayed bitter
Then I couldn't grow"

Scromlette then whipped
up some omelets for all.
Because kindness always wins,
Even if the giver is small.

Special Thanks

Nancy Arendt
Nancy Christensen
Wes and Michele Christensen
Tim and Meaghan Ciochon
Stephen Papstein
Nathan Little
Jose Nuno

About the Author

Zach Christensen obtained his Bachelor of Arts in Sociology and Communications from Doane University. Zach enjoys creating stories to illuminate young minds, and asking questions that allow for new ways of seeing the world. Zach resides in Lincoln, Nebraska.